Gladys

the Grayish-Green Dragon

Gladys

the Grayish-Green Dragon

by Ben Utter

Illustrated by
Hannah Lloyd Rosell

Bowen Press

www.BowenPressBooks.com

Published 2017 by Bowen Press
A project of the Dunbar Group, LLC
Tyler, TX 75703
www.BowenPressBooks.com

ISBN 978-0-9994729-0-3

Printed in the United States of America

Original illustrations by Hannah Lloyd Rosell

For Serena and Thomas,
whose fires are never out

"My teeth are all brushed (eighty-seven, I counted)

With Dragon Breath Toothpaste, the perfect amount," said

A high little voice from a high little bed,

Where Gladys the grayish-green dragon, instead

Of hiding at bedtime, her usual habit,

Had tucked herself in before mother could nag.

And it wasn't because she was tired from doing

A day full of dragony things like ha-*choo*-ing

Twin fountains of pink and blue fire from her snout.

(Though that sort of thing would tire you, have no doubt!)

Nor was it for beauty she'd curled up to rest;

Being beautiful's one of the things she did best!

Her scales weren't red like the dragons of China,

But old gravy gray-green, a color that's kinda

Like lima beans *plooped* fresh right out of a can,

Swimming shiny and cool on your plate or your hand.

And it wasn't because she was worried her dad

Would thump his great tail on the floor and look mad

As he had yesterday, when for almost an hour

Gladys refused to take even one shower!

(Most dragons take seven—and ten in July!

If you've ever smelled one, you'll understand why.)

"Not even a drizzle! Not even one drop!"

She had said to her stern-looking mother and pop.

"I do not like bedtime! Not even an ounce!

I will not set claw on my bed but to bounce!"

Father looked thoughtful. He sighed and said, "Glory!

We've tried everything. I have told every story

That I've ever known and a few that I don't,

But nothing will get you to sleep—you just won't!

"So tomorrow I want you to go on to bed,

And if you're especially good, then instead

Of turning your light off and hoping you're quiet,

I'll bring an old dragon sleep trick, and we'll try it."

And so on *this* night Gladys showered eight times,

Neatly folded her wings along parallel lines,

Polished her scales to a Dragon Wax bright,

And gargled to put out her fire for the night.

(Next morning at breakfast, of course, she'd reverse this

By lighting a match and hiccoughing on purpose.)

And when she at last was all settled for sleep,

Her father said, "Ready? Let's try crunching sheep!"

He brought in a whole wooly flock to her bed.

(Just where he had got them he never quite said.)

"Oh yes!" Mother said. "Crunching sheep is quite nice.

You'll go right to sleep. Take your father's advice."

Gladys was grateful, but hated to eat

So soon after brushing her six rows of teeth.

So she said, "I do hope you won't think it bizarre

If I just want to see first how many there are.

"One, two, and three sheep," she said, and then, "four."

She began to say "five" but instead she said "*snore*."

It broke with tradition, but Gladys was right,

For *counting* sheep put her to sleep every night.

So now you know Gladys, and now you know how

Dragons came to count sheep. Why don't you try it now?

Ben Utter is Serena and Thomas's dad and Brandy's husband. After living and teaching in China, he earned a PhD in English with a minor in medieval studies from the University of Minnesota. Dragons, sad to say, featured prominently in neither of these endeavors, though he continues to keep a hopeful eye out for any who might be lurking in the shrubbery (or sleeping in class) at Ouachita Baptist University, where he is an assistant professor of English.

Hannah Lloyd Rosell is an illustrator, teacher, and artist. She earned a BFA in painting and MAE in art education at Truman State University and now passes on the joy of art to her pre-kindergarten through eighth grade students. Along with her artist spouse, Bryan, Hannah has settled into the home of her heart, Kansas City, Kansas. There she enjoys raising chickens, gardening, and spoiling her pet rats, cat, and puppy.

CPSIA information can be obtained
at www.ICGtesting.com
Printed in the USA
LVIC06n0047090118
562349LV00007B/12